Really
Rabbits

Virginia Kroll • Illustrated by Philomena O'Neill

✺ Charlesbridge

To my pets' sensational vets, Drs. Robert Rogers, Sharon Fisk,
Carl Tomascke, Claudia Cataldo, and Susan Mercer. — V.K.

For Paul, who I Really love. — P.O.

Text copyright ©2006 by Virginia Kroll
Illustrations copyright ©2006 by Philomena O'Neill

Published by Charlesbridge, 85 Main Street, Watertown, MA 02472
(617) 926-0329 • www.charlesbridge.com

Library of Congress Cataloging-in-Publication Data

Kroll, Virginia L.
  Really rabbits / by Virginia Kroll ; illustrated by Philomena O'Neill.
       p. cm.
  Summary: Two pet rabbits sneak out of their cage at night to tidy the
house and do other chores so that their owners will have more time to play
with them.
  ISBN-13: 978-1-57091-897-1; ISBN-10: 1-57091-897-X (reinforced for library use)
  ISBN-13: 978-1-57091-898-8; ISBN-10: 1-57091-898-8 (softcover)
  [1. Rabbits--Fiction. 2. Housekeeping--Fiction.] I. O'Neill, Philomena,
ill. II. Title.
  PZ7.K9227Rea 2006
  [E]--dc22
                        2005020405

Printed in Korea
(hc) 10 9 8 7 6 5 4 3 2 1   (sc) 10 9 8 7 6 5 4 3 2 1

Tulip the bunny waited every day for Grace the girl to come home from school. Then Grace would take Tulip out of the cage, stroke her silky fur, and play with her.

Tulip didn't like being alone every night. She was lonely most of the day too. When Peter the boy brought a fluffy gray bunny home one day, Tulip thumped for joy.

Snuggle was grumpy at first, but he and Tulip
soon became great friends.

Together, they told rabbit jokes and played
rabbit games.

One night, during a game of Rabbit Round
the Rosy, Tulip got an idea.

"Every day, I see how Grace opens and closes
the door to our cage. I think I might be able
to do it!"

Tulip stretched her paw through the cage and lifted the latch. *Presto!* The door swung open.

"Come on, let's go!" she said.

Tulip raced here, and dashed there, and did flips in the air. Snuggle scurried across the carpet and slid across the floor.

They found treasures everywhere.

"Yum!" said Tulip. "A piece of celery from Grace's dinner!"

"And here's a raisin from Peter's snack!"
said Snuggle.

In the morning, an alarm clock rang loudly.

The rabbits hurried back to the cage when
they heard footsteps on the stairs.

Night after night, Tulip and Snuggle escaped and explored.

Soon, they had visited every room in the house.

They wanted to try something new.

"I have an idea!" Tulip said one night.

She and Snuggle got busy folding all the
clean bath towels in the laundry basket.

Next morning, the children's mother
smiled, "How nice! I thought Peter
would forget to do that."

The next night, Tulip and Snuggle washed the dishes.

The night after that, they swept the floor.

Another night, they put the toys away . . .

and dusted the furniture.

The next night, they neatly lined up
the shoes in the back hall.

The children's mother said, "How nice!"

She gave each child a special kiss before they left for school.

One day, Grace raised her eyebrows at Peter.

"Mom sure is happy. I wonder who's been cleaning up."

"Maybe it's elves," guessed Peter.

"Or fairies," said Grace.

"Thank you, whoever you are!"
Grace shouted, hoping the helpers
could hear her.

Tulip whispered, "They always think magic
is done by tiny people."

"They'd never believe it's really rabbits!"
agreed Snuggle.

The next night, Tulip and Snuggle stacked the magazines and newspapers to be recycled.

"You know, our cage could use a cleaning," said Snuggle.

"No way," Tulip said. "It's more fun to clean Grace and Peter's house. Besides, then they'd know it was us!"

So instead, Tulip and Snuggle
cooked a tuna casserole.

Grace and Peter's mother was happier than ever.

"Delicious!" said their father. Grace and Peter agreed.

The whole family smiled more and argued less.

Best of all, Grace and Peter had more time
to play with Tulip and Snuggle.

One afternoon, the children's mother said, "Why don't you let your rabbits hop around and explore a bit? They must be tired of sitting all day."

Tulip and Snuggle tried to hide their smiles.

That night they turned on the computer
and looked up ways to make carrot cake.